The Aloe Trap

for Naomi Rose Shaw, 1989–2006

Kate Rhodes

The Alice Trap

ENITHARMON PRESS

First published in 2008
by Enitharmon Press
26B Caversham Road
London NW5 2DU

www.enitharmon.co.uk

Distributed in the UK by
Central Books
99 Wallis Road
London E9 5LN

ISBN: 978-1-904634-64-5

ACKNOWLEDGEMENTS

Some of the poems in this collection have been published in: *Agenda, Coffee House Poetry, Interpreter's House, Magma, Mslexia, New Writing 15, Poetry Monthly, The Rialto, Smith's Knoll.*

Thanks to the organisers of the Speakeasy Competition 2005, the Ilkley Festival Competition 2005, the Church Urban Challenging Poverty Competition 2007, the City of Derby Competition 2007, and the Bridport Competition 2007 for permission to republish the following prize-winning poems: 'The Movement of Bees'; 'The Package'; 'The Instant Husband'; 'Portrait of My Husband as a Lightbulb'; and 'Wells-next-the-Sea'.

I am indebted to the Society of Authors for a bursary awarded to me in 2007. A number of poems in the collection were written during a fellowship at Hawthornden International Writers' Retreat.

With thanks to Dave Pescod, Helen Johnson, Elizabeth Foy, Sarah Shaw, Jessica Penrose, Mandy Green, Cambridge Women Writers, Cambridge First Tuesday Poetry Group.

Designed in Albertina by Libanus Press
and printed in England by
CPI Antony Rowe, Chippenham, Wiltshire

CONTENTS

The Alice Trap

Everyone I've Ever Known

The Memory Club

The Alice Trap

THE ALICE TRAP

I was unprepared.
By the time I saw you
I'd forgotten the Alice traps
hidden in the ground,
narrow enough for a girl
or a thin woman to slip into.

You made no attempt to save me.
My fingernails snagged
on polished walls,
pictures went by like prompt cards –
tureens, diamonds and knaves,
rabbits tall as princes.

You saw me crash
through every landing
into a jabber of unknown sounds.
I landed in your lap, ribs bruised,
only your Cheshire Cat grin
to warn or welcome me.

BEGINNING

We forgot to eat, or look outside.
Weeks went by without landmarks,
our clothes littering the stairs.

Your odd house sheltered us,
remote and singular
keeping itself to itself,

peering above the lip of the fen,
like a sheepdog cowering
or an infant's first tooth.

THE PLOT

I try to picture it as you do,
the home you plan to build
swaying above us,
house martins flitting between the eaves.
But the walls quiver, see-through as windows,
nothing here but immovable weeds –
long swags of brambles,
mare's tail in hairbrush spikes.

Your face tips back, eyes so blue
the sky has poured itself into them.
You're completely absorbed –
checking the angle of lintels,
positioning each slate.
You've already turned the key,
watched nightfall paint itself
across the bedroom floor.

THE FAMILY VISIT

You brought me to this place
when we were still afraid to go anywhere
without touching – especially here,
Scots pines denying the light,
patches of bluebells refusing to be cowed.

You showed me where you used to play
inside a hollow oak, hidden behind monuments.
This was your starting point,
the ivy tangling fenland dynasties
keeping you in your place.

Your sister's here already;
dead in her teens she's been praying
a long time for a visit from you.
Her headstone lists backwards
as if she hopes someone might catch her.

Your mother and father
are so close they're almost touching,
respectable in grey marble,
holding their peace, for all the world
as if they had never hurt anyone.

SWEETHEART

When I called you that, you flinched.
It made me wish I'd covered myself,
told you that where I come from
shopkeepers throw the word out
easily – a kiss goodbye
from someone you hardly know.
But I missed my chance,
watched your discomfort sharpen
as the consonants soured on my tongue.

PERMISSION

We spent our time together
happy and speechless,
ignoring the phone,
co-ordinating our breathing,
pressed thin by the weight of touch.

Come to think of it
you hardly ever met my eye,
too busy reading my skin,
studying it like a script
you had to learn that day, by heart.

We didn't leave each other much,
just the invisible ink of deleted emails.
But I can't help remembering
the way you handled me –
your dry-fingered lack of delicacy.

I can feel the pressure sometimes still –
your thumb against my collarbone.
I feel it now. But I still don't know
who gave your memory permission
to touch me, when I try to sleep.

THE PACKAGE

I listen to your goodbye
without taking off my coat.
Your voice crackles with certainty.

No need to play the message twice.
I hunt for brown paper, scissors, glue,
if I work fast nothing will be lost.

Not the way you held my face
turning it to the light,
a precious stone you had to value.

Not the weight of your hands
tethering me to the bed,
their restraint natural as gravity.

The package will be sealed
so light can't touch it,
safe on the table in the hall.

Then you will have said goodbye
and I will have said, look,
it is not destroyed.

If you don't believe me
I will post it to you.

THE MOVEMENT OF BEES

The park looks different today,
every flower shrieking with brightness,
fabulous technicolor certainty
that I will see you again.

I will watch you sleep.
When I touch your face
you will smile, reach up
trap my fingers in your hand.

Maybe you're home already
waiting for me upstairs,
unpacking your bags.
I have to stop myself from running.

The breeze has dropped,
but in the rose garden
blossoms are dancing, petals jittery
with the movement of bees.

DETAILS

The inventory is almost complete,
exact and alphabetical,
a catalogue of objects you touch –

your favourite porcelain cup,
magazines you forget to read,
a dozen shirts waiting to enfold you.

In your study I check the plants
you grow from seed,
struggling on the windowsill.

Tonight I will spend hours
calculating how much air
you need each day to breathe.

If I take a break
I will lose my command.
Details will begin to disappear,

even the colour of your eyes –
an exact match for the sea
on the first day of winter.

THE PARKING SPACE

The radio's stopped working.
No company in the car
except words reciting themselves
from a medical dictionary –
erotomania, de Clerambault's syndrome.

The truth is, you're not coming back,
you're staying with your wife.
But it's enough to be close to the place
where you always parked your car.
I watched you every day

reversing through the narrow gate,
looking over your shoulder,
muscles tight across your neck,
as if you were scared already
of what the mirror might see.

I WILL NOT THINK OF YOU AT 4 A.M.

I will use lists as my defence,
each item a stone in the barricade
keeping you in your place.

The easiest come first –
capital cities, Shakespeare's heroines,
male names beginning with S.

You hover over me
waiting until I relax or forget,
fingers drumming on the bedside table.

I'm running out of categories:
dog breeds, prime ministers,
lovers who left me, lovers I left,

footballers with unusual names,
English counties, types of cheese.
Nothing helps.

You're waiting for me
in the contents of rock pools,
blond hair mingling with anemones' tendrils.

SINGULARITY

Surely it's meant to be easier?
Not so much self-pity,
less of a shock when the sheets
are clean and cold and unforgiving.

I expected peaceful afternoons,
time loose around me
to watch the twist of shadows,
the tamarisk's feathered leaves.

But all I see are the spaces
between cups on the dresser,
gaps I never registered before
between the kitchen tiles.

I turn the radio on, but pauses
announce themselves between notes.
Soon the players will abandon
their instruments, set light to their scores.

FOUR THINGS YOU NEVER GOT TO SEE

My new attitude –
chin up, nothing dents me.
Oh yes, I'm doing fine, thank you,
in my jacket of impervious leather.
That table, please, the one by the window.

The town I've borrowed
shot through with privilege and dirt.
Tourists like ice cream wrappers,
littering themselves across the common
as far as the eye can see.

The haircut that cost a fortune,
blonde, high maintenance.
It makes a Jean Harlow of me,
sends me on errands for sequins,
bon-bons and dancing shoes.

The underwear I bought
just before you left,
held together by willpower.
Red silk daisies, faces to the sun
blooming in a field of lace.

Everyone I've Ever Known

AURORA BOREALIS

For one lesson only the science teacher
allowed himself to rhapsodise.

The Northern Lights, his eyes blurred
like a telescope gone wrong.

When you see them
it makes you believe the sky's singing.

Everyone laughed. But now they're above me
making a mockery of learning.

Someone is scratching a fingernail
across the night sky. Under layers of soot

between pinpricks of stars,
a child's painting is burning through.

PLANETARIUM

The heavens turn on at 8 p.m.
Last show of the day –
two thousand light-bulbs
masquerading as galaxies.

Fornax, Cassiopeia and Pegasus,
candyfloss swirls of Northern Lights.
But when I close my eyes I'm back
in that winter, when the power cuts took hold.

Candles came to life in windows
one by one, as if we lived in a softer world.
We lay on the grass swaddled in coats,
studied astronomy by torchlight.

It took weeks to learn the constellations.
Until then they'd been hard to find,
the city hoarded them
inside a mantel of polluted light.

When the strikes ended they disappeared.
Maybe the circuit-board was broken,
or no one remembered
to flick the switch.

THE ANGEL GATE

It stands at the edge of the dunes,
splintered and worn by too many tides.
The key turns reluctantly,
mechanism stalled by salt and cold.

They're impatient today, crowding me,
breath chilling the nape of my neck.
A flock of them jostle me from the path,
not flying but running.

Latecomers race to catch up,
bare feet skidding on the boardwalk,
preoccupied, muttering to themselves,
reciting lists of things not to forget.

Their music disturbs me as I count.
It's my job to keep track of them
without meeting their eyes –
blindness is an occupational hazard.

When the last stray feather
has been collected
I'm off duty, until dawn
when the next shift arrives.

REASONS TO VISIT A CATHEDRAL

Sixty-five per cent
said they made a special trip,
travelled long distances
in search of history and calm.

Thirty-one per cent
came by chance, lit candles
to familiar superstitions,
dropped coins into the box.

But four per cent couldn't explain.
Maybe it was Jonah's instinct
on a December afternoon,
to hide inside the whale?

Some of them were drawn here,
to study the marble patience
of the retriever sleeping
at the saint's feet.

Or perhaps they only needed
to stand alone in the transept,
watching a miracle of light
smash down in coloured pieces?

THE STOPOVER

The city is giving nothing away.
It could be Hong Kong, or Singapore
pretending to be Tokyo.

Clouds pass in slow motion,
drawing continents of shadow
on the wall beside my bed.

Just for today there are no boundaries.
Grey archipelagos shift and settle
as the afternoon ages.

Even the old worlds
refuse to stay the same,
reinventing themselves as new.

Islands uproot themselves,
territories colliding like icebergs
or disappearing between fault-lines.

THE HOROLOGIST

X-ray clear, from the north,
his workshop fills every morning
with the best light for repairs.

Instruments wait for him on the bench –
stereoscopes, examining pins,
tannic acid to strip rust from steel.

Each day the clocks are dusted,
Ingraham and Bulle
kept apart like warring tribes.

Ranked on the shelves
they are stubborn and unwilling,
beating decades instead of seconds.

They know they're in danger.
Tomorrow he will remove
first their faces, then their hands.

CAFÉ AT THE V&A

For Elizabeth Foy

This is your writing place,
hidden in the basement between dusty brick walls,
a clutter of uncomfortable chairs.
But it sells the good coffee you insist on
and in some ways it's like you –
no pretences, face to the air
on a raw Norfolk beach, back turned
as if you wanted to keep the sea to yourself,
monopolise the breakers and the gulls.

It's not hard to picture you here
in your expensive second-hand coat
surrounded by chatter, completely absorbed,
words insisting themselves onto your page.
One floor above you the gods and goddesses
of the Hindu and Jain are being admired,
their gold mouths open in surprise,
as if the kingdom of heaven
had suddenly flung open its doors.

ANNE LISTER'S DIARIES, 1806–1839

There's no freeing you.
You've padlocked yourself
in these tight books.

In the coded woods of your diary
birds, crow-like and sinister
flock the margins.

Reaching into the mirror
you took the face of a nobleman.
Only two paths being available

you chose the hazardous one,
shingled your hair,
longed for a clever wife.

The gossips christened you
Gentleman Jack, hissed
at your handsome face.

Numbers, symbols, Latin, Greek,
kept you corseted
from genteel disapproval.

You wrote yourself a shield
for the man's fragile body,
hidden inside your skin.

FOR CALLIOPE

I sent them away,
the same young men as before
with their parchments and their greed.
They're waiting by the river,
watching the ships go by
as if life was nothing to them
but leaving and arriving.

It makes me angry
the way they tire you, make your voice
weak as the June breeze.
I've warned them not to rely on you –
one day you will take your own journey.
There will be no more monsters then,
or rescues, no more good deeds.

Don't cry. They will come back.
They'll be here by dawn tomorrow
begging for romance and bloodshed,
ambushing your heroes.
But today you must rest.
Smell the lavender I hid under your pillow.
Sleep if you can, without dreaming.

FOR GEORGIO MORANDI

Every day you copy them
bottle, plate and bowl,
rough-skinned earthenware
crackle-glazed with age.

White as your winter face
they glow like familiar ghosts.
The bowl mouths at you,
begs for a last crumb of sun.

A neighbour visits unannounced.
She burdens the plate with bread,
ladles scalding soup into the bowl,
force-feeds the bottle with vinaigrette.

You wait for her to leave
before rescuing each piece.
Tomorrow you will hide them,
tuck the key inside your shoe.

FIRST LIGHT

Just after midnight
I hear the sea curl against the land to sleep,
the wind bedding down between beach huts.

A gaggle of boys pass the house.
Some nocturnal disappointment makes them drag
a chain of metal sounds behind them.

Keys ice skate across bonnets,
wing mirrors crunch underfoot,
but first light cancels out teenage noise.

By dawn my neighbour is kneeling in her porch,
preparing to scrub night-time to extinction
with the hard bristles of her brush.

VERTIGO

The ceiling tips onto my pillow then rights itself,
and I start that climb again
to the lighthouse platform at St Augustine.

A chain of strangers links behind me,
filigree steps too narrow
to accommodate second thoughts.

Through slotted windows
buildings uproot themselves,
streets dance between neighbourhoods.

Far away Cape Canaveral glistens.
Boats rise close to my face then fall back
onto the bumpy picnic cloth of the sea.

I grab the rail, try to steady myself
with the thought of astronauts
shooting unafraid into a vertigo of stars.

THE LAST NEW ROMANTIC

Between May and August
young men were allowed to be pretty.
Decked out in ballet-dancer lace
they pliéd by the railings,
catwalked the High Street
dragging scarves of *Miss Selfridge* gold.

His skin bloomed
under make-up and silk.
Gangs of lady-boys crowded him,
reeking of *Anaïs Anaïs*.
All summer long the radio yearned –
we know this much is true.

By autumn the fad was over. '
Crew cuts make a comeback,
lace and frills were abandoned.
Only he refused to change,
immaculate and geisha-mouthed,
alone in his seaside town.

FLAMENCO

My neighbour is practising again,
notes stumble past me when I try to sleep.
He sits by the open window –
a big man, curled into himself, eyes closed,
cradling his guitar awkwardly
like someone else's child.

The instrument looks comical,
tiny as a banjo against his bulk,
but some days he makes dancers appear,
spinning and stamping
across the wooden floor,
onyx and lace glittering in their hair.

I watch them through the crack in the door,
pray they won't see me.
The men are the eye of the storm,
women's skirts whipping around them.
When his music finishes
they disappear back into the walls.

A safety net of brambles
chokes the path to his front door.
This evening I must find a way
to leave my gift – four peaches,
in a blue-glazed bowl from Madrid,
ripening all night in his porch.

THE INSTANT HUSBAND

I found you by the side of the road.
You gave me directions,
your mouth level with my eyes.
Turn left at the war memorial, you said.
Or stay here, have a drink,
be my wife.

We were married before I had time to blink.
Before I knew your blood type, or next of kin
or your occupation: fisherman.
It's still hard not to be afraid.
Things that start fast
end fast, my mother said.

But each day when you come home
you smile, as if you'd known me all your life.
I walk to the harbour to make sense of it.
If I look hard enough I can find your boat
held up to the sky, at rest
on the sea's wide palm.

PORTRAIT OF MY HUSBAND AS A LIGHT BULB

If I sit close enough, I can read my book by him,
static crackling in his Einstein hair.

Floorboards scorch under the soles of his feet,
no one can short circuit him.

Comforting as a kettle boiling in another room,
white noise hums inside his skin.

Ideas fine as filaments ignite behind his eyes
but by midnight he's waning. Moths ignore him.

When we lie down to sleep it is possible
at last, to admire him without shading my eyes.

HUSBAND AND WIFE

They keep their backs to the mirror
cast shadows thin as pencils,
separated by candlesticks and ornaments,
last month's anniversary cards.

One foot in front of the other
he carries a spear, matchstick wide,
prepared to walk forever if necessary
back to the Cape.

She refuses to be distracted
stares out of the window at passing cars,
elongated arms heavy
with bangles of ivory.

Neither has aged
since they travelled here,
choking on tissue paper
in my suitcase from Johannesburg.

And they haven't changed their minds.
Square-shouldered, heads high,
they still take in the world
through narrow, chiselled eyes.

THE METAL BIRD

You used to pretend you could hear
the lorries drumming by,
but only their pulse came to you
through the soles of your feet.
You could dance using the same trick –
Sinatra's words escaped you
but not his beat.

Silence wrapped you
in concentric circles,
bullying you behind a sound-proof wall.
The last time I saw you
I dropped a vase on your stone floor.
You didn't flinch as the water
lapped the backs of your shoes.

You were watching a blackbird,
beak gaping at the quiet
where song should be.
We used to watch the metal bird together.
We could both hear it, Concorde heading west,
cracking just for one moment
the sound barrier.

MY FATHER NEVER WENT OUT

Except to work, and when he came home
work came with him –
requisition forms to fill out
in triplicate, by yesterday.

His pen traced ghost words in the air
before the courage came to start.
We pulled faces behind his back,
goggled at the TV.

He stood by the door letting in draughts,
barked at us every day
to keep our shoes off the carpet
he slaved all year to earn.

The box was mindless nonsense
except for his favourites:
Steptoe, Hancock, Rising Damp.
He watched the repeats on his own.

We could hear him through the door
laughing at men he recognised –
unsuccessful with women, overlooked,
eyes brimming with dreams.

ANGLE-POISE

Misunderstanding the laws of nature
my father places himself

under a direct light,
hoping to dissolve by morning.

But the beams do nothing
except warm the roof of his mind,

bring his anxiety to a simmer,
brightness fizzing in his ears.

It reminds him of Sunday school angels
who wore their haloes

tipped at dangerous angles,
as if they wanted nothing more

than to fall back to earth,
render themselves human again.

On the wall ahead he sees
the outline of the lamp's crooked arm

and himself – a blurred thumbprint
on a circle of gold.

MISSING PERSONS' BUREAU

I came here to find my father
but the faces on the wall are not my father's.

I show the interviewer letters, bills, a bank statement,
he shuffles forms. *How long since you saw your father?*

Fourteen years. He takes off his glasses, puts down his pen.
What kind of daughter waits so long to find her father?

This man must be dutiful. Christmases and outings,
golf every Sunday to please his father.

But I'm not going to leave. I might still find him –
filed away, name forgotten, waiting to be my father.

CROSSES

I see you working in the train's silver window
head bowed, nodding,
with your chisel and your mason's glue.

Behind you small towns vanish,
chapels and terraces run an endurance race
down granite hillsides to the sea.

At Aberporth your house is full of crosses
cut from wood, limestone, slate,
patterns scratched under their skin.

Saint George tattooed on a scrap of willow,
scales bitten from the dragon's back.
Stories chasing the grain of agate.

At the wake an old woman
tells me of your last discomfort,
pressing her closed face into mine.

My inheritance arrives by post,
a Celtic knot wrapped in visions
library books refuse to explain.

THE YEARS

I remember you before they locked you up.
The way you shook them off,
steered their sniffer-dogs down the wrong alley,
laughed as their crashed cars burned.

I remember you before they tracked you down.
The way you flirted with them,
made them fawn on you
with Cat Woman's lipstick snarl.

Last time I saw you, it was all their fault.
Eighty of them had you surrounded.
It was a conspiracy, they kept you trapped
in a wheelchair prison,

forced you to sit and count the days.
Lines had been painted on your face
and worst of all, they made you watch
when they threw away the key.

But this time there was no getaway car,
no boat to speed you to St Tropez.
*There are too many of them, you said,
one false move and they'll blow me away.*

EVERYONE I'VE EVER KNOWN

They come out of the woodwork.
Old flames smoulder in the kitchen,
gaggles of schoolgirls circulate
with drinks and crisps.

Mrs Keller arrived at nine.
She's trapped upstairs with my boss,
he's ruining her beehive hair,
her best kindergarten dress.

In the living room my grandmother
gobbles ice cream, mutters to herself.
My ex-husband is true to form,
in the garden with the postman's wife.

My father waits by himself
outside in the Morris,
listening to *Book at Bedtime*,
trying to keep warm.

He's afraid of crowds.
But when everyone leaves
maybe he'll knock on the door,
apologise, make amends?

THE LOST MOUNTAIN

A curtain of beads hangs across the door.
Rosa walks through as if it didn't exist
talking of her father, lost to Franco's war.

Men came for him at night, marched him away
until he was claimed by the bend in the road.
From the balcony she can see the gap

where the mountain used to stand –
Monte Perdu, highest peak in Ordesa,
sides quarried raw as wounds.

Home to no one except priests and goats,
it hung above the village, protected
through the seasons by its wrapping of snow.

A band of clouds came for it last winter.
Now Rosa is more vigilant, keeps a notebook,
records the temper of the sky.

Who knows what might be taken
if she shuts her eyes? Nothing is safe,
not even her garden or the village school.

THE CONVERSATION

They make it clear from the start
they're reasonable people.
All I have to do is listen,
be honest, give straight replies.

Soon the conversation will end
but there's no need to be afraid.
They leave me paper,
one silver pen for company.

Just one hour to record
every detail I can think of –
numbers, safe houses,
the codes I memorised.

Keys rattle questions in the lock.
Unlikely as a zeppelin
the pen is distended,
almost certain to implode.

REMEMBRANCE

We use our helmets to shield our eyes
from starlight and flares,
but it's no use. Even in silence
something keeps us awake,
lodged in our minds, painful as shrapnel.

In seventy year's time
even our youngest will be gone.
No one left to speak for us
although speech hurts him, a flake of rust
in his mouth in place of a tongue.

AL-MUSAYYIB, 16TH JULY 2005

The houses are all the same,
low walls and shuttered windows.
Hard to imagine how the villagers survive –
scratching seeds into dust,
the desert singeing their heels.

Cars pass like seconds, never pausing.
The children are always busy,
boatbuilding from nothing
except rags and sticks and dreams,
sailing yachts across oceans of sand.

The bomb was planted before dawn,
blankets of shrapnel glittering on the road.
A soldier from Alabama was killed outright,
nothing left to send back home.
The defence say his friends stopped thinking.

They kicked down the schoolhouse door.
The children were completing a test
heads down, remembering the alphabet,
pencilled letters marching right to left
in neat, unfinished lines.

GOODBYE, MR PRIME MINISTER

A cartoonist has redrawn your eyes
made one a pinprick of cunning, the other
telescope wide, focused on nothing.

You're on the front page too, prematurely old
like a veteran who fears another war.
It's hard to remember why the tabloids fell for you.

Maybe it was your caught-in-the-headlights stare,
or that tremor a voice coach taught you
to make you sound sincere?

We must have been gagging for promises –
education, education, education.
You could have fed us

any line three times over
like a mantra or a spell,
we'd still have swallowed you.

The Memory Club

BELONGINGS

My friend is losing her daughter by increments.
Small things have gone missing already –
energy, the brightness of her skin.

In the meantime she's ordinary,
shielding herself against jargon:
anaemia, myeloid, acute.

Wandering from shop to shop
it's a struggle to choose her winter coat.
Fashion decisions last all afternoon.

She goes home with bruises under her eyes
but happy, half-asleep in the car,
carrier bags full of mohair and silk.

Tomorrow when her strength comes back
she'll parade the length of her room –
new dresses, bracelets, high-heeled shoes.

I won't let myself imagine her mother
kneeling by her bed, alone,
sorting her belongings into piles.

I SHOULD HAVE BOUGHT YOU THOSE
BOOTS WHICH COST A FORTUNE

You stood by the shop window, worshipping them.
You didn't say *I want them* or *buy them for me*
but I should have done.
I should have led you inside,
watched a swarm of assistants fuss over you,
admiring your long, slim calves.

Those boots would have been a ticket to happiness
for a whole afternoon. I see that now,
and I see that I should have treated you more.

But I made the same mistake as always,
following the echo of my father's advice –
a penny saved is a penny gained,
forgetting that bank notes are just a background
for the queen's unchanging face,
mysterious and precise, filthy with use.

WELLS-NEXT-THE-SEA

Two months, they said
or with luck factored in, up to a year.
By then you'd abandoned luck,
decided to throw a party immediately.

It would last all weekend
in your favourite place –
a gaggle of caravans
hidden behind the dunes.

We waited for guests in our tin box,
rain clog-dancing on the roof.
It took two boxes of matches,
the best part of an hour, to light the fire

and I wanted to tell you
I can't do this. I can't celebrate
knowing you, then losing you
before you've even finished school.

But you were lolling on a pile of cushions
head back, listening to the sea.
Come and sit by the mirror, you said.
I'm going to show you

how to do your eyes.
You'll see how easy it is,
and when I'm finished
you won't know yourself.

CELLOPHANE

Your mother called last night,
warning me not to bring flowers.
You're sick of them. Acres of rustling plastic,
and that smell they leave
of nature giving up the ghost.

Your room is shrink-wrapped in cellophane,
pillar-box red gerberas, hot pink roses,
as if you could make a gift of hope
vivid enough to transmit itself,
turn out to be a cure.

I have brought you a shawl instead.
You will wear it each day until you die,
the fabric softer than rain –
grey, slub-marked silk,
so understated it scarcely exists.

THE PICNIC

Bumpy as a crocodile's back,
the table you made carries
Spode, Wedgwood, Poole,
lodged in its resin skin.

It's heavy with food and words today,
a resting place for bottles of Pimms,
oval plates loaded with sandwiches
and condolences.

The breeze steals our memories,
drops them to the crazed ground,
until rain pelts us with silence.
We salvage almost everything –

wine glasses, strawberries,
photos of you.
Sheltering in the porch
we watch the storm tear

white petals from the clematis,
handle them roughly,
hurl them to the floor
like plates at a Greek wedding.

THE DOUBLE-TAKE

You're standing outside *Top Shop*
surrounded by girlfriends –
in the thick of things as usual,
wearing a cool Kate Moss hat.
You look at ease, fully recovered.
I try to catch your eye,
almost raise my hand to wave.

But you are only you for a moment
before I have to double-take you
back into my memory. It doesn't seem fair
to lock you inside on such a sunny day.
You're only asking for one more afternoon
of gossip and bargains,
trying on dress after dress.

PAST PERFECT

I'm fighting with Voltaire today,
struggling to remember 'O' level French
and the teacher who terrified me –
Miss Guillaume with her chignon,
her sharp Parisian suits.
She used to scrawl verbs on the board,
shriek at us until we understood.
Past simple, pluperfect, future conditional.

For you the future is without conditions.
You will not finish learning French.
You will not become a photographer,
get married, or travel the world.
You are confined to the past perfect:
you loved cocktails, parties and old films.
You stayed up late, even when you were ill.
You danced for as long as you could.

THE MEMORY CLUB

Maybe you know this already
but your friends have started a memory club.
They get together after school,
watch your favourite soaps, talk about you.

They have bought small, white gold hearts
to hang on chains around their necks
with your name inscribed on them.
They have given one to your mother.

Your best friend is exhausted.
To her you are a physical absence.
She still wears the jeans you gave her.
Eating pizza reminds her of you.

Teachers keep asking how she is.
None of them understand that you
are something she needs every day
but cannot have, like a missing tooth.

AFTERLIFE

Your parents scattered your ashes
in the places you loved most –
Southwold beach, the Deben at low tide,

under the great oaks in Christchurch Park.
But the trouble is, I can still see you,
right on the edge of adulthood, waving at me.

I'd like to join you just for an hour,
watch you clowning to Radio 1,
the whole of your childhood still in view.

But if I had to describe where you are now
I'd vote for Joni Mitchell every time –
we are stardust, we are moonlight.

Tonight when I look at the sky
I understand what she means. It's not hard
to picture you, glittering there.